Hailey's Dream
by
Jennifer Kuhns

Illustrated by Patty Burgi Sneed
Illustration assembly by Jennifer Kuhns

Hailey's Dream

For information contact: Shalako Press
P.O. Box 371, Oakdale, CA 95361-0371
http://www.shalakopress.com

ISBN: 978-0-9846811-8-1

Cover Design: Jennifer Kuhns
Cover art and illustrations: Patty Burgi Sneed
Illustration Assembly by Jennifer Kuhns
Formatting by Karen Borrelli

:

PRINTED IN THE UNITED STATES OF AMERICA

Hailey's Dream

Hailey Burke was a little girl in a wheelchair. She was in a wheelchair because she was born too early. Her brain didn't have enough time to grow all of the way, so some of it didn't work. The part that told her legs how to walk didn't work. So, Hailey used a wheelchair to get around. Her friends thought it was cool to not have to walk all of the time. They thought she was lucky.

Hailey didn't think she was lucky. She really wished she could walk like all of her friends. They got to run and jump and climb on the jungle-gym. Sometimes it made her really mad or really sad that she couldn't do any of those things.

One night she was so mad and sad about not having legs that worked right that she went to bed very early and told her mom that she was never getting up again, ever.

Hailey woke up and rolled over. When she opened her eyes she looked right at a girl with black hair and green eyes standing by the side of her bed. "Who are you?" Hailey asked the strange girl.

"Hi, my name is Miranda," the girl said. "Won't you come play with me?"

Hailey liked meeting new people and having friends. Even though her mom always told her not to talk to strangers, she figured that her mom knew Miranda because she let her in the house, and into her room.

"Sure," Hailey answered, forgetting she was sad and mad. "Where are we going?"

"Follow me," Miranda said.

Hailey threw back the covers to get into her wheelchair and was surprised to see that she didn't have legs anymore.

Instead of legs she had a big yellow and green fish tail. "What happened to my legs?" Hailey asked Miranda.

"You don't need legs to come play with me," Miranda said. "We all have fish tails where I live."

Hailey looked down where Miranda's legs should have been. Instead of legs she saw a beautiful, sparkly red and gold tail.

Hailey started to get out of bed and noticed that she was already floating. Her bedroom was full of water and Miranda was wiggling her tail back and forth. Miranda was a mermaid.

"Woohoo," Hailey shouted as she wiggled her tail back and forth like Miranda. "I'm a mermaid too! Now I bet I can do everything!"

Miranda and Hailey swam out through an open window.

Hailey expected to see her backyard. Instead, she saw sand, and seaweed, and pretty shells, and lots of different colored fish. She even saw a swimming turtle.

"Are we swimming in the ocean?" Hailey asked.

"Yes we are," answered Miranda. Just then another mermaid swam up to greet them. "This is my brother, Addicus, and his dog, Marley. They want to play, too."

Addicus had a blue and black tail that glittered when he moved it. Hailey didn't want to be rude and stare. She knew it wasn't polite, but she couldn't help staring at his dog, Marley.

He was half dog and half fish. He was a dog-fish.

Hailey smiled at Addicus and Marley, and asked, "How exactly do mermaids play?"

Miranda and Addicus each grabbed one of Hailey's hands. They gently pulled her along, close to the bottom of the ocean floor, being careful not to let her rub her tail on the sand and rocks. It wasn't long before Hailey was swimming all by herself.

"Wow," Hailey said excitedly. "This is the first time I have ever moved without my wheelchair." Then she began to spin and twirl, and dip and dive. She was having the best time, ever. She had never felt so happy. She didn't need her wheelchair as a mermaid.

When Hailey decided that she knew how to use her tail as well as Miranda and Addicus, she wanted to know everything else about being a mermaid. She wanted to know what mermaids did. Did they go to school? Did they have chores? Did they have to be in bed by eight o'clock? But that could wait. First, she wanted to have more mermaid fun.

Miranda and Addicus spent the rest of the day showing Hailey what mermaids did. They swam, of course. They played tag. They played hide-and-go-seek. They chased smaller fish. They explored ships that had sunk to the bottom of the ocean.

They made seaweed and coral necklaces. They swam and played with dolphins. They even played fetch with Marley by throwing a sea shell for him to find.

All the playing was making Hailey hungry. "What do mermaids eat?" Hailey finally asked.

"We eat plants," Miranda answered.

"Oh, okay," Hailey said. "What kind of plants?"

"Well," Miranda said. "We eat all kinds of plants. I guess you would call them sea plants. Here, try one."

Hailey wasn't sure if she wanted to eat a sea plant. She watched as Miranda and Addicus both munched on the leaves of a slimy olive green plant. She decided to be brave and try it.

First, Hailey took a tiny bite of the plant and chewed it up. Then she took a bigger bite. "Humm," she said. "It tastes like brussel sprouts." It wasn't pizza, but Hailey decided sea plants were good enough to eat, and her mom would like that she was eating vegetables without being told.

After eating what Hailey thought was probably lunch, she watched as Miranda, Addicus, and Marley stood straight up on their fish tail and began to gently swish it back and forth. When they were done, they had each made a hole in the sand just big enough for them to curl up in.

"So, what are we going to do now?" Hailey wanted to know.

"What do you mean?" Addicus asked.

"I mean, what are those holes for?" She answered.

Addicus made another hole next to the first one he had made. "This is where we are going to sleep," he explained. "This spot is for you."

Hailey didn't understand. "I don't take naps anymore," she said. "I'm too old for naps."

"We aren't taking a nap," Miranda said. "This is how we sleep for a long time so nothing bothers us while we are sleeping. See, nothing can see us."

Hailey watched as Miranda, Addicus, and even Marley, swam around and around in small circles until they floated down into the holes.

When they all stopped moving, Hailey could see that the three of them looked just like big rocks lying on the bottom of the ocean.

Hailey wondered why Miranda and Addicus didn't live and sleep in one of the ocean caves they had played in today, or maybe even in one of the sunken ships. She thought those would have made really cool places for mermaids to live.

In fact, Hailey wondered if they had any kind of home at all. She wondered where their mom and dad lived or where they kept all of their stuff. She really didn't know if Miranda and Addicus even had a mom or dad. She didn't know if they had any kind of stuff at all to keep in a house. Hailey decided that there was a lot about being a mermaid that she didn't know. So, she settled down in her own hole in the sand and thought about all the questions she wanted to ask her new friends.

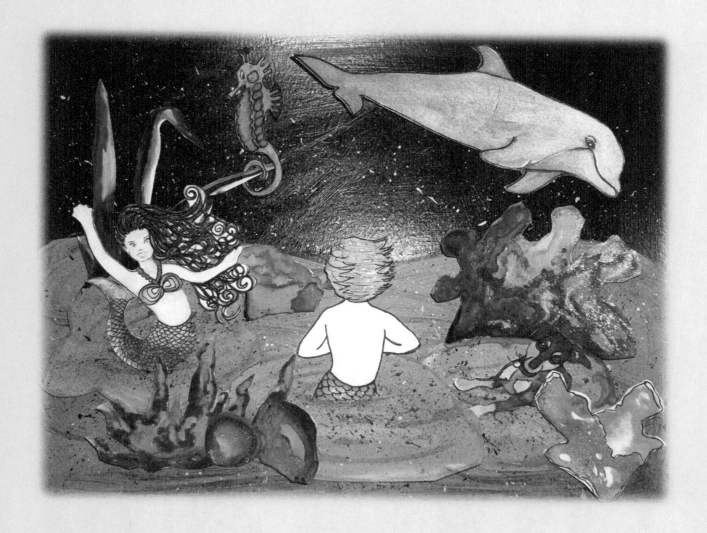

It seemed like forever before her new mermaid friends woke up. There weren't any clocks in the ocean so Hailey didn't know what time it was or if it was even day or night. She did know that she had to find out what else mermaids did. It was fun being a mermaid and playing all the time, but Hailey thought playing all of the time would probably get boring because things would be the same every day.

Before the mermaids had a chance to stretch and get the sleep out of their eyes, Hailey asked, "What are we going to do now?"

"What do you mean?" Miranda asked.

"I mean, what else do mermaids do besides swim, and play and eat," Hailey said. "Don't you have to go to school? Do you have to go home and do chores? Do you have a mom and dad or a house to live in? Do you ever read a book or write a letter? I mean, where I come from I do all kinds of things even though I have to use a wheelchair."

"Read or write," Miranda said. "What does it mean to read and write?"

Hailey was very surprised. "You know, like with paper and pencil."

Both Miranda and Addicus looked at Hailey confused. Miranda answered Hailey's questions.

"We are mermaids. We live in the ocean where we don't need legs to get around. We swim and play and explore all day long, and if we want to all night. That's what mermaids do. Didn't you want to be where you didn't need legs or a wheelchair to get around?"

Hailey thought for a very long time. "Well, not exactly, Miranda. I did wish that I could get around without my wheelchair, but I didn't want to be a fish. I wanted to be a person who had legs that worked. It was fun being a mermaid for a little while, but I miss being able to help my mom cook dinner, and wearing cool clothes, and painting my fingernails, and e-mailing my friends, going to school and painting and writing, and SHOPPING.   I have to be able to go SHOPPING!" Hailey gave a big sigh. "I miss my family and friends and eating pizza and ice cream and singing. I even miss doing my chores because I like having something important to do.

I like having lots of different kinds of things to do and learn. I really just like and want to be ME. I think it is more important for me to be me in a wheelchair than me in a fish tail."

Miranda and Addicus swam around Hailey and gave her a big hug. "I suppose you are right," Miranda said. "Will you come visit us again?"

"Of course I will," Hailey answered. "But next time I come to visit I'm going to have an orange and purple mermaid tail with silver sparkles. If I'm going to be a fish, I'm going to be the colors I like."

Suddenly, Hailey heard music coming from somewhere. When she opened her eyes she was back in her bedroom. Her wheelchair was parked next to her bed where she had left it the night before. She reached and turned off her iPod and could hear her mom in the kitchen making breakfast just like always.

"Wow, what a weird dream," Hailey said out loud as she pulled back her blanket to get out of bed and into her wheelchair. "It might be cool to be able to move like everyone else, but it is *definitely* cooler being able to do all the other things that I can do, even in a wheelchair."

The End

Dedication

In memory of

Dr. Armin Schulz (Bob to me)

October 17, 1946 ~ April 30, 20ll

My friend, my mentor, who confirmed that I could do anything.

He was the biggest supporter of children's literature,

and collector of over three thousand children's books

which now comprises the

Armin R. Schulz Children's Literature Collection.

ALSO BY JENNIFER KUHNS

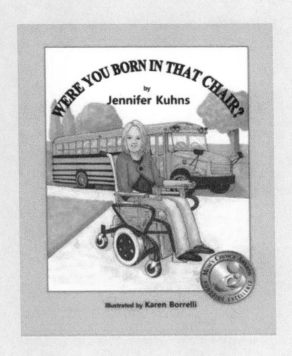

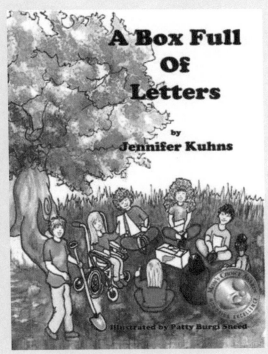

Shalako Press

http://www.shalakopress.com

CPSIA information can be obtained at www.ICGtesting.com
Printed in the USA
LVOW021008290413

331354LV00007B/13/P